Wolf

by

Tommy Donbavand

Illustrated by Dan Chernett

To: Zohrna, Ellisha, Jamie, Lewis,
Courtney, Shane, Salula, Ellise, Calum,
Charlie, Bethany, Finley, Alex, Liam H,
Aiden, Levi, Blake, Liam C, Erynn, Sonia
and Danielle

First published in 2011 in Great Britain by
Barrington Stoke Ltd
18 Walker Street, Edinburgh, EH3 7LP

www.barringtonstoke.co.uk

ISBN: 978-1-84299-483-2

Printed in China by Leo

Contents

Chapter 1
Claws

I reached under my pillow to grab a chocolate chip cookie from the half-empty pack and stuffed it into my mouth in one go. Then I flicked off the pause button and went on blasting zombies on my new Playstation game.

The tips of my fingers were hurting a bit. Perhaps I'd been playing this game a bit too long. Or maybe I was pressing the buttons too hard. I decided to take a break when I got to the end of the level.

I bit into another cookie, making sure to brush any crumbs off the bed covers. I was really hungry tonight – but I knew my mum would go mad if she found out I'd sneaked a packet of biscuits up here. She said every room has its own use and if I wanted to eat in my bedroom, then I might as well start sleeping in the dining room.

The zombies on the screen kept up their attack. My character in the game had a baseball bat in his hands and was bashing their heads in with it. They gave a moan each time I hit them, but I made sure to keep the volume low as my dad was downstairs reading the paper, and I didn't want to disturb him.

My mum and dad can be a bit strict at times, but there's always a good reason for their little rules and, so long as I stick to them, I get a treat every now and then – like this new game.

My fingers were really sore now, so I pressed pause again to take a break. My hands felt hot and stiff. I could see the lines of the veins in my palms. What was going on?

I was about to call for my mum when the first claw ripped through the end of the middle finger on my right hand. It slid right out of the end, ripping my own finger-nail off and spurting blood all over the bed. My mum was going to kill me when she saw this mess!

Another claw sliced through my skin – this time, the thumb on my left hand. I stared in horror at the long, sharp, yellow talon, still dripping with blood. My nail hadn't been torn off all the way this time and it hung, attached by a flap of skin, above the claw.

My shock gave way to pure panic and I don't mind telling you that I screamed – loud and long. I was terrified.

By the time my mum and dad came to the door of my room, I had three more claws on my fingers and two had ripped through the ends of my toes, right through my socks. It was a good thing my mum made me take my shoes off as soon as I got home from school.

"Adam!" my mum gasped. I turned towards her. I was crying. Tears were streaming down my face as another talon tore its way free of my fingertip. I wanted to wipe the tears away, but my hands were soaked with blood and I didn't want to put my fingers too close to my face in case I did any more damage.

Then my mum buried her face in my dad's chest and said something I really didn't expect to hear. Something that chilled me to the bone. "It's started!" she sobbed. "It's started to happen!"

For a moment, I forgot all about the pain in my hands and feet, even though the last remaining claws were slicing through the skin and ripping away my nails. "What do you mean?" I asked in horror. "What's started?"

My dad came to kneel beside the bed, leaving my mum crying in the doorway. She

couldn't look at me. He pulled the pillowcase off my top pillow and began to wipe the blood from my fingers, ignoring the packet of chocolate chip cookies now plainly on view.

"It's OK," he said softly, rubbing my hands clean. "We've known for a long time that this might happen, but we're going to deal with it." He carefully pulled away the two fingernails still attached to my skin, then turned to remove what was left of my socks from my blood-soaked feet.

"What is it?" I asked. "What's happening to me, Dad?"

He looked back up at me and I could see his eyes were wet with tears, too. "Adam," he said as calmly as he could, "you're changing into a werewolf."

Chapter 2
Fur

I saw the light from the full moon shine through the window as my dad led me carefully into the bathroom. Could he be right? Was I really turning into a werewolf? Ten minutes ago the worst thing I had to worry about was biscuit crumbs on the bed covers.

"We need to get you cleaned up," said my dad as he turned the taps and started to fill the sink with water. Every room has its own use – even when you live with a monster. I sat on the toilet seat. My mum stood in the doorway, but she still couldn't look at me.

My hands and feet hurt like hell. Blood was starting to clot around the torn skin of my fingers and toes. My dad dipped a cloth into the warm water and began to wash it away. For some stupid reason, my dad being so nice to me made me want to cry again.

"Werewolves aren't real!" I said, fighting back tears. "Werewolves aren't real!" I don't know who I was trying to convince more – myself or my mum and dad.

No one said anything. The only sound was the splash of the blood-red water in the sink as my dad dipped the cloth in again. My leg felt itchy, but I didn't dare scratch it with my new claws, so I rubbed it with my elbow.

"What's going to happen to me?" I asked.

My dad kept on washing me. "I don't know," he said in a low voice. "But I don't think this is the end of it."

I felt my heart thump in my chest. "You mean other bits of me will change?"

Before my dad could answer, my mum spoke up. "We don't know that!" she said. "It could stop after this." I don't know why she seemed so angry. It wasn't as if I was doing this on purpose.

Then a thought came into my head. "How do you even know about this?" I asked. "How did you know that I was becoming a werewolf?"

My mum and dad looked at each other again. This time, however, my mum looked scared rather than angry. I itched my chin with the back of my hand.

"Werewolves are real, Adam," my dad said firmly. "Your mum and I have known about them for a long time."

"But how – " I began.

My dad stopped me. "It's not something everyone knows about – most people think they're just in comics or films. But, when you've got one in the family ..." His voice trailed off into silence.

"Then why doesn't it affect you or Mum?" I asked. "If this is something that happens to our family, then why have I never seen either of you change?"

My mum made a sound like a low sob. I didn't dare look at her in case it started me crying again. Instead, I tried to focus on rubbing my heel against the annoying itch on my other shin.

My dad sighed. He suddenly looked a lot older than before. When he spoke, his voice was very quiet. "Because we aren't your real parents," he said. "We adopted you."

For a few seconds, it felt like the bathroom was spinning around me and I almost fell off the toilet.

"You're not my mum and dad?"

My mum scowled. "Of course we are!" she snapped. "We've given you a much better life than that pair of ..."

"That's enough!" my dad shouted.

Silence filled the bathroom again. I began to scratch madly at my chest with my new claws. They were good for something after all.

"Your real parents died when you were a baby," my dad continued. "We – your mum and I – we took you in, and ..."

He stopped, watching me. "What's the matter?" he asked.

"I'm itching all over!" I moaned, scratching harder than ever. Suddenly, my long claws ripped through the thin material of my school shirt and it tore away. My dad gasped and I looked down.

My chest was covered with thick, brown fur.

Chapter 3
Tail

I pulled off what was left of my shirt and stared at myself in the bathroom mirror. My belly, chest and shoulders were covered in thick, dark fur, and the stuff was beginning to creep up along my arms and hands.

My shins were itching too, so I quickly tugged off my school trousers and stood in only my boxer shorts. Within seconds my feet, legs and knees were hidden under a layer of dense fur, each hair forcing itself through my skin.

By the end, the chocolate brown fur crept up my neck and began to cover my face. There wasn't a razor in the world that would be able to shave this amount of hair. The funny thing was, once I was covered from head to toe, it didn't itch anymore. It did feel like I was wearing a thick dressing gown, though.

If I hadn't been so scared I would have laughed. It had to be a joke. First of all I started growing claws, then I found out that my mum and dad aren't my real parents, and now I look like a walking teddy bear. Someone, somewhere, was having a good laugh at me.

I was red hot under all that fur and the heater in the bathroom was switched on full as usual. I had to get out of there and cool down.

I staggered out onto the landing and leant back against the wooden railings at the top of the stairs. As I passed my mum, the fur on my side rubbed against her bare arm and she pulled away from me with a squeal. My eyes flicked up to meet hers and, for a moment, I wasn't sure who she was. I shook my head and told myself it was just because my mind was confused with everything else that was happening.

It wasn't as hot on the landing, and I took a few deep breaths to try and calm myself. "Did they have to go through this?" I asked.

My mum, still standing in the bathroom doorway, with her arms folded, looked puzzled. "Did who have to go through what?"

"My real parents," I said. "Did they change like this?"

"We don't know," said my dad as he pulled the plug out of the sink and watched the swirling, dirty red water vanish down the drain. "We didn't know them that well."

"You must have known them a bit," I said. "They did give you their baby."

My mum choked back a laugh. "If only it had been like that," she sighed.

My dad threw her a look and stepped out onto the landing beside me. "They had to give you up rather quickly," he said, looking away from me. "There wasn't really time to get to know them – as people, that is."

There was another cold laugh from my mum. "People ..." she muttered.

My back was pressed hard against the wooden railings and I shifted my weight a little. "OK," I said. "What were their names?"

My dad was quiet for a moment. "Like I said, we didn't really know them ..."

"Maybe not," I argued, "but there must be information somewhere, about where I was born and who my parents were. If I can find out more about them, maybe I can learn how to stop this!" I was starting to lose my temper. The lower part of my back was really sore, and neither my mum nor my dad seemed to want to give me an honest answer.

"I might have family," I said, bending forward to try and ease the pain that pounded in my back, at the bottom of my spine. "Aunts or uncles – other werewolves who could teach me how to – "

"No!" my mum shouted. "You're one of us now – not one of those ... those animals! You'll have nothing to do with them!"

I felt the anger build inside me. "But I need to find out if I can – " I fell forward as the pain in my spine suddenly exploded. Inside I felt the muscles in my back stretch and grow, twisting around themselves to form a thick rope that forced its way over the top of my boxers. Fur swept down over the length of skin, covering it within seconds.

I had grown a tail.

Chapter 4
Snout

My mum gave a shudder and turned away. I stayed where I was, on all fours, and glared up at her – my tail swishing from side to side.

"I will find my real family," I growled. "You can't stop me."

"There's no need to be rude," my dad said, taking my arm and helping me to my feet. "Your mum's just trying to look out for you."

"Look out for me?" I gasped. "You've said nothing to me about any of this for years! Then, in one night, not only am I a werewolf, but I'm not even your son!"

"Of course you're our son," my dad said, giving me a hug. He didn't seem worried about touching my fur, although he flinched a little as my tail flicked against his leg. I wasn't really sure how to keep it under control yet.

I pressed my furry face against his chest and closed my eyes. I could hear his heartbeat in my ear, and it made me feel safe. I began to cry, and could feel tears trickle through the thick hairs on my cheeks. "Who am I?" I whispered.

I could tell from the way my dad was breathing that he was crying, too. "You're Adam Heath," he said softly. "You always have been, and you always will be."

After a moment, I opened my eyes again, hoping that it was all over and I'd be back to normal. It wasn't. I still looked like I was half dog.

Suddenly, an idea came to me and I pushed myself away from my dad. "The Internet!" I cried.

"What about it?" asked my mum sharply.

"They have all sorts of information online," I said. "I'll bet there's a website where you can find out about birth records!" I began to run down the stairs, feeling hopeful for the first time since this nightmare had started.

"You can't use the laptop," my mum said firmly. "It got a virus and the hard drive died. I have to take it in to be repaired."

"That's OK," I said. "I'll use the computer in dad's office."

"You will not!" shouted my mum.

I stopped, halfway down the stairs. My nose was twitching and I could feel my face begin to stretch out into some kind of snout. I gritted my teeth against the pain as my bones cracked and reshaped themselves and tried my best to ignore the long whiskers pushing out from the clumps of fur on my cheeks.

"But there's a computer in the office," I repeated. "I might be able to find some answers ..."

My mum had her don't-mess-with-me face on. "You are not to go anywhere near that room!" she shouted.

I sighed. I'd never been allowed inside my dad's office. It was always kept locked and he never talked about what he did when he was in there. I knew there was a computer inside, however, because I'd once seen my dad coming out with some holiday booking emails he'd printed off.

Every room has its own use – and this one was so my dad could get away from his family.

Just like he did when he went on those long fishing trips without me.

My face was shaped like a wolf's now, and inside my mouth a long tongue lolled from side to side. It made talking difficult, but I gave it a go. "Why are you doing this?" I asked. "Why won't you let me find out about my real family?"

My mum stood her ground. "Your father's office is off limits, young man!"

With my new nose, I could smell all sorts of odd things from around the house. I knew there was an old sock somewhere under my bed, a rotting banana skin in the kitchen bin, and there was something else ... Something I'd never smelled before – but I knew instantly what it was.

It was fear. My mum was scared of me!

This is stupid, I thought. If she'd just give me half an hour on the computer, I might be able to find a way to change things back. Then she wouldn't need to be scared!

I made up my mind to use the computer in my dad's office whether she liked it or not. I leapt down the last few stairs and ran along the hallway to the closed door next to the downstairs loo. I didn't know where the key was kept, but maybe I could break the door open or even use one of my long claws to pick the lock.

As I grabbed the door handle I heard footsteps behind me and felt cold steel on my neck as a metal dog collar was slipped round my throat.

Chapter 5

Eyes

My dad clipped a thick dog lead onto the collar and tugged me away from the office door. The metal chain pulled tight around my throat as he dragged me along the hall with all his might.

"What are you doing?" I gasped.

"Your mum told you to stay away from my office!" he shouted.

The sharp claws on my feet scratched at the polished wooden floor as he pulled me into the front room. The dog collar was one of those ones that closed tighter the more you pulled on it. It was so tight around my throat that I thought it was going to choke me.

"Please ... stop!" I begged.

But my dad didn't stop. He yanked on the lead as hard as possible, tightening the collar even more. My mum stood behind him, staring at me in horror as though she was looking at some kind of monster. I don't know what upset me more – the look on her face, or the metal chain closing in around my neck.

"This is for your own good," my dad said firmly.

"But ... it's hurting me ..." I hissed. "And why have you got a collar and lead? You never let me have a dog ..."

"We've had it for a while," replied my mum. "Just in case this happened. In case you started to change."

This was like some sort of nightmare. Not only was my body changing in ways I could never have thought possible, my parents were now treating me like an animal in order to stop me finding out what was really going on.

I took a step forward. "Dad, please ..."

My dad didn't answer. Instead, he wrapped the dog lead around his fist and pulled even harder.

Then he began to change. He went all blurry for a second and, as he came back into focus, he looked different. His skin had turned pale yellow and he looked – well, he looked like he'd taste delicious.

I turned to look at my mum. She too had a yellow glow to her and her bare arms seemed to be asking me to bite into them. They looked as tasty as the fried chicken we'd had the night before.

It took me a moment to realise that my parents hadn't changed at all – it was my eyesight. I glanced up at my reflection in the living room window, and was surprised to see my eyes had changed shape. They were wider now, and a deep yellow in colour. Thin black slits ran down the middle of each eyeball.

I turned round and stared at my parents. They stood out from everything else in the room. The walls, furniture and plasma TV seemed to fade away into the background. They had lost all their colour and looked as though someone had painted them grey.

But my mum and dad – they looked wonderful. In fact, it was hard to take my new eyes off them. Any bare skin glowed pale yellow and I could almost see the hot, sticky blood pumping through their veins.

My tummy rumbled.

My dad must have heard it because he gripped the lead in both hands and pulled the collar even tighter around my neck. He looked scared and – through my new eyes – that just made him appear better tasting than ever.

I would never hurt my parents, though, and I tried to tell my dad that but the choke chain was now so tight around my throat I couldn't speak. I began to feel dizzy and my tongue hung loosely out of the side of my mouth. I knew it wouldn't be long before I would stop being able to breathe. I had to loosen this collar.

Reaching up with one of my paws, I sliced through the lead with one of my long nails. My dad fell back against the fireplace, pulling my mum down with him. The pain on my throat went away and I bent forward, taking long, rasping gasps of air in an effort to fight off the dizziness.

Feeling better, I stood up again and turned to make my way back to the office. If I could just get onto the computer, I was sure I could find out how to stop this. How to stop my mum and dad being so scared.

I heard footsteps and spun round to find my dad coming towards me – a metal poker from the fireplace gripped in his hands like a weapon.

Chapter 6
Spine

My dad brought the metal poker down hard on my right shoulder and a lightning bolt of pain ripped through my arm – much worse than anything I'd felt before.

"I told you to stay away from my office!" my dad yelled.

Why was he doing this to me? I would never hurt him or my mum. I just wanted to find out more about what was happening to me and if there was anything I could do to stop it.

I tried to tell them that I loved them, but all that would come out was a deep growl. It sounded like I was snarling at them.

The poker came down again, hitting my leg this time. My dad's face was twisted in a mixture of fear and rage. His teeth were gritted and his cheeks red.

He attacked me for a third time – the poker hitting my left arm. Suddenly, I reacted. I lashed out with one of my paws and scratched his cheek with my sharp claws, leaving four streaks of blood behind.

He staggered back, clutching at his face and with blood all over his hand. At once, I felt bad for hurting him, but there was another feeling inside me now as well – another feeling pushing the guilt away. I lifted my claws to my mouth and lapped my dad's blood from my talons – and then I knew what this new feeling was. It was hunger. The raw hunger of an animal. I had tasted blood, and now I wanted more.

The werewolf inside me was starting to take over.

I knew I had to try and keep hold of myself. I may look like a walking monster on the outside, but I was determined the animal instincts would not take control. I tried to think of the most boring, down-to-earth things I could and started running through them in my mind.

My name is Adam Heath. I live in England with my mum and dad. My mum belongs to a book club and reads lots of yucky romance novels. My dad goes fishing for the weekend every month or so.

My name is Adam Heath …

I could hear my thoughts ringing inside my head as though they were being pushed to one side by something more powerful. The wolf was battling with me, trying to take charge. Trying to force any memories of Adam Heath into the darkest corners of my mind.

My name is Adam ...

For a second, I couldn't remember my last name, and it scared me. If I could remember who I was, then I wouldn't be a real werewolf. I could stop the change and go back to being plain old Adam ... Plain old Adam ...

I had forgotten my last name!

I had to get to a computer while I could still remember how to use one. The library would still be open at this time, but I didn't think the neighbours would enjoy the sight of a half-formed werewolf plodding down the street. Plus, now I was almost naked and covered in fur, there was nowhere to put my library card.

I had to use the computer in my dad's office and I ran back towards the locked, white door. Just as I reached it, my mum brought the plasma TV down on the back of my head and I fell sideways into the kitchen, splinters of glass puncturing my skin.

And then my spine snapped in half.

Chapter 7
Teeth

I'm pretty sure my spine snapped completely in two then came back together. At least, that's what it felt like. I lifted my snout and howled in agony as the pain shot down my back and wrapped around my belly.

My claws dug into the expensive kitchen floor and I screamed to my mum and dad for help – but all I heard was the slam of a door, and the turn of a key in the lock.

Then I felt the muscles in my back begin to rip apart. No, not just feel them – I could hear them as they tore apart. It was like the sound your knife makes when you're cutting through your beef at Sunday lunch – only much louder. It was horrible.

And as if the pain in my back wasn't bad enough, I felt my gums tear open as long, razor sharp teeth burst through. It was a good job I wasn't able to speak any more as I now had thick fangs filling my mouth. I would have sounded totally stupid!

I was in agony, and I thought I was going to die. I really believed that the change had gone too far. I wasn't just becoming a werewolf – my body was breaking up into little pieces and I would never change back. The last thing I would ever see was the kitchen floor and what was left of the shattered TV set.

The lower half of my body shifted as my muscles pulled in tighter together. They gathered around my reshaped spine and

hunched me over, moving my legs closer to my arms. No – they weren't arms anymore. They were two front legs.

I had four legs. I thought, *this is going to cost my mum a fortune in shoes.*

Then, just as quickly as it arrived, the pain went. I lay, panting on the kitchen floor in case the agony returned, but somehow I knew it wouldn't. In fact – not only was I sure the hurting was now over, I felt incredible.

I climbed up onto all four feet and padded across the kitchen. I arrived in the hall and looked around. To my surprise, I could see streaks of yellow hanging in the air in front of me – as though someone had painted brush-strokes onto a piece of clear glass. I suddenly realised that I wasn't seeing the smears of colour – I was smelling them.

My senses were more powerful than ever, and I could use my nose to follow the path my parents had taken after my mum had hit me with the TV. They had run along the hall – and gone into dad's office.

After all that stuff about me not being allowed to go in there, they'd done just that!

I felt the rage deep inside me. I would get them for this. I would rip their –

No! I wouldn't do anything like that. I may now be a fully-formed werewolf, but I'm not a monster. I pushed the wolf-like instincts to the back of my mind and made them stay there. I would never hurt my mum and dad, and I had to let them know that.

My claws clicked against the floor as I made my way to the office door. The handle looked yellow with my dad's scent and I reached up with my front paw to try and turn it – but I couldn't get a grip on it. So I scratched at the wooden panels, scraping the paint away with my claws.

"Go away!" bellowed my dad from inside. "I'll kill you if you come any closer!"

The fur on the back of my neck rose up in anger. There was no way I was going to let my prey kill me. When I got in there I would clap my teeth around that human's throat and –

Stop it! I am not going to hurt anyone – and my dad's not really going to hurt me. But then why did he say he was going to kill me? Didn't he realise I was only trying to let them know I wouldn't harm them?

I had to get inside that office and tell them that I was still me. That I was still ... still ... Damn! Now I couldn't even remember my first name!

I rose up on my back legs and threw my weight against the door. The lock gave way at once and the door crashed open. My mum and dad were backed up against the far wall of the room and, in the dim light, I could see that my dad was struggling to load a shotgun, with his fingers trembling.

Where would my dad have got a shotgun? I'd often wondered what it would look like inside his office, and I thought it would be filled with fishing rods and books about carp and trout. But this was nothing like that.

Shelf after shelf was filled with the heads of dozens and dozens of dead animals, with even more staring down at me from the walls above. My dad hadn't gone fishing when he was away after all. He'd been hunting ...

I froze as something caught my powerful eyesight. There – on the wall above my mum and dad – were the heads of two werewolves. Two werewolves that looked exactly like me.

"I'm sorry," my mum sobbed. "We couldn't have children of our own, and I wanted a baby so much! I really thought we'd have longer with you ..."

I heard the click as my dad finished loading the shotgun. He aimed the twin barrels straight at me.

With a final glance up at the sad, lifeless faces of my real parents, I let my human self go and allowed the werewolf take over the last remaining parts of my mind.

Then I pounced.

Barrington Stoke would like to thank all its readers for commenting on the manuscript before publication and in particular:

Akshay Aggarwal

Daniel Allen

Hartej Anand

Dylan Barlow

Aimi Bleasdale

Joshua Blows

Xarius Dalal

Aaron Fayinka

Jacob Lucas

Lucy McGee

Zak Mustafa

Jack Oliver

Alexander Peck

Bailey Pick

Megan Pollard

James Sweetlove

Krzys Tytko

Jack Warder

Have you read Tommy's other books yet?

Zombie!

Nathan thought he knew all about zombies.
They're dead.
They like eating brains.
But he didn't know they liked to party.
Until he met Jake. Jake's been dead for 60 years and his arms keep falling off – but that doesn't stop him having a good time.
This party's sure to be a SCREAM!

The Uniform

Matt's got a problem. The school bully has picked him as his new victim.
It looks like it's game over for Matt.
But then things start to change. *He* starts to change.
He isn't afraid anymore.
He has the power.
Can he control it?

More fab books from Barrington Stoke

The Fall
by
Anthony McGowan

Mog might be a loser, but he's not as much of a loser as Duffy. So when Duffy tries to get in with Mog's best mate, Mog decides to take action. But when he lands Duffy in The Beck, the rancid stream behind school, Mog has no idea how far the ripples will spread...

Bad Day
by
Graham Marks

Rob's going to meet Tessa.
Like, for real.
In person.
For the first time.
Then Rob starts to think twice. And what should have been a great day begins to fall apart, big style...

You can order these books directly from our website at
www.barringtonstoke.co.uk

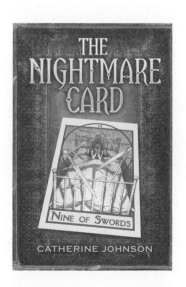